A BAKER'S DOZEN

Thirteen short stories about everyday life for you to read and enjoy.

By Mary T Bradford

A Baker's Dozen

By Mary T Bradford

Copyright Mary T Bradford © 2011

This book is a work of fiction. Names and characters and any resemblance to actual persons, living or dead, are entirely coincidental.

This book is licensed for your personal enjoyment only. All rights reserved. No reproduction, copy or transmission of this work may be made without written permission from the author. Thank you for respecting the author's work.

TABLE OF CONTENTS

Introduction by Mary T Bradford.

Room 103.

A Secret Farewell.

The Coffee Morning.

A Family Broken.

Always A Choice.

A New Start.

Coal Dust Is Gold.

Anonymous.

Ivy Close.

Would Mother Approve?

Mystery Customer.

Beneath the Surface.

A Sunbeam.

Introduction

Hi Readers, my name is Mary T Bradford, the T is for Theresa! I have been writing short stories for many years. I have enjoyed publication in various magazines, newspapers and anthologies, (both Irish and USA). I have completed my first novel, *A Thorn in My Side* and have started on my next book.

I hope you enjoy the stories in this book and thank you for choosing my work.

You can read more on my blog http://marytbradford-author.blogspot.com/

ROOM 103

'On the morning he disappeared he had followed his usual routine' were the words that Frank read in the Daily Post. He allowed himself a chuckle or two as he munched his marmalade and toast. He was overwhelmed with the enormity of interest that had sprung up resulting from his disappearance. Frank read on, the article outlining how he always cut the lawns of his semi-detached on Saturday mornings and went for his walk afterwards returning to his house at midday.

The neighbours said how quiet and helpful Mr. Frank Bosworth was, never interfering, but there if you needed him. Each neighbour had given a little story about how he had been a friend of the missing man thus getting their fifteen minutes of fame. Truth was, Frank had very much kept to himself and the most neighbourly act he carried out was giving a pint of milk to Mrs. What's her name at number 16 when one of the kids had knocked on his door. But as he read on he remembered more, the time he got the kitten stuck up a tree down for the toddler across the road, another time how that fellow two doors up couldn't start the car and Frank had helped with his jump leads.

Four days now Frank was officially missing. Four days his neighbours and friends were worrying about him, his family were scattered abroad. He thought it would be easy to disappear. Now sitting in the luxury hotel room with breakfast served to him, Frank was confronted with the reality of his life. He did have people who cared so why had he been pushed to just up and leave his home in Primrose Avenue?

Lying back on the cool sheets, he stared at the chandelier in the centre of the ceiling. Each piece of glass or was it plastic glistened in the morning rays. The room was full of sunshine, the large windows allowing the eastern sun to drown the room in light.

Frank sighed. He was tired. He had his reasons for wanting to take time out. The past few months had been harrowing for him. Maybe if he had confided in one of his work colleagues or even a neighbour. After all a problem shared is a problem halved. Well that had never been his way, but this could be a new beginning, a time for change. Right now though he would go for a sleep and he could deal with his thoughts later.

Sleep had now become a luxury for Frank. Most nights he paced his house trying to find a solution to the mess he was in. Here in the hotel, he slept soundly. The difference was amazing, just physically being removed from his home allowed him to enjoy deep undisturbed sleep, so far. But sooner than he had planned Frank would have to face up to the depths of debt he was in. Staying in his room he felt safe from temptation, it sounded so easy to tell himself this but the reality was so different.

Life had taken such a nasty turn that coping was the challenge, it was the largest risk he ever faced. Frank showered. Standing in front of the bathroom mirror he shaved. Each stroke as the razor cleared the foam, revealed to Frank the face of a troubled man. The recession was to blame; this climate of cutbacks and levies applied by the government was crucifying people like Frank. That was it!!!

He didn't need Gamblers Anonymous. Where had that idea come from? But looking deep into the eyes of the man in the foggy mirror told him differently, they told the truth, no recession was the reason for Frank's problems. It was the constant on-line gambling, the chances that were too good to refuse flashing on the screen, the promise that everyone walks away a winner, no-one leaves the poker table a loser. Hours sat in front of this compelling playmate had cost Frank more than money.

 His house was on the line. He had already pawned his watch, stereo music system even his new plasma TV just to have cash to pay bills. Food and work had become secondary in his life. His weight had plummeted from skipping regular meals although lately, the worry of where his next cash flow would come from had added to his thin appearance.

 Coming to this hotel was his cold turkey. Just a week here without going out would help him recover. It worked for others, alcoholics, drug addicts, often their stories were in the media, and how they locked themselves in rooms and faced their demons. So Frank took himself off to the hotel and requested no computer or access to and no TV in the room and by keeping himself indoors for the week, it would help him sort his life. But truth be told, Frank was struggling. Reading about the worry his neighbours and friends were going through was reassuring to Frank in an odd way. The daily paper delivered to his room was the only link to the outside world with the crossword providing some mental challenge.

Franks debts were high into the thousands on just his credit cards alone. He had gone to a loan shark to borrow cash to pay for the hotel. Now that was trouble Frank would face on the weekend. Larry who dealt in backstreet banking would be looking for his first repayment on Sunday next.

Sitting by the window watching people pass up and down, he wondered what troubles they carried on their shoulders or were they all living happy families? Reading the latest article again, he wondered when he had made friends with his neighbours. Never had he invited them into his home, nor had he showed interest in their daily living, yet he was a part of their world. Someone out there had reported him missing. Someone out there in Primrose Avenue cared about him. A bit freaky Frank thought but yet touching. Maybe he wasn't the loner he made himself out to be. What if he were to talk to someone, really talk. Not just silly neighbourly chats but tell them his whole sorry mess that his life was. How dark and lonely the future ahead of him waited. Right now its only greeting was one of doom and beatings from Larry's boys.

    In his haste to escape from his home he had overlooked explaining his absence at work, was he really in so deep that the thing in his life that occupied most of his daylight hours had not even taken up a minute of his thoughts? This mess was destroying all he realised and he had to beat the evil that his gambling had grown into. Right now he didn't fancy his chances of seeing this week through, definitely he wouldn't be a safe bet. A safe bet, good choice of words, Frank laughed out loud. Acknowledging his own failure was a tiny step but important and laughing at his own stupidity for letting his life go belly-up, made Frank feel in control. Control that he had and not the poker table or silly bingo, which made him sit in front of a screen each evening and often late into the night. He continued to laugh, he even did a little skip around the dull brown carpeted room, his laughter growing as he twirled and spun until he soon began to cry. Tears hot and salty splashed his face, his nose snotty as he gulped for air, between sobs. Falling to the floor he hugged his knees to his chest and how he longed for just one more chance, just one good hand at the card table and he could end this misery.

The evening grew dull and the sun grew low in the sky so only shadows crept across the room and kept Frank company. He pulled the duvet around him and lay on the floor. His body trembled and shuddered. The aching for the bright computer screen promising a royal flush was flashing in his mind. His blood pumped around his body in search of the adrenalin rush he got when an ace came his way. Now it was starting, the clammy sweat on his forehead dampening his hair and Frank wrapped the duvet tighter and buried his head into his chest as pain of withdrawal teased each sense in his body.

He couldn't do this alone, he would need support. He would have to accept help but tonight he would see through and never forget the lesson he would learn from this. The tears were now tears of relief, the darkness outside would bring a new dawn and Frank would start a new man, broken but not forever. He would go home. He would ask for help and he would be a better neighbour and workmate, maybe even help out at Gamblers Anonymous. Curling up on the carpet Frank slept fitfully, the hardness of the floor a reminder of the tough times ahead. The luxury of the hotel lost as he lay there.

****

A SECRET FAREWELL

She thought of her journey over, how, when looking out of the carriage window, it started to rain, the drops scattered at first, and then falling steadily. Tracy's mood had matched the drabness of the day. Watching the rain, she had distracted herself from what lay ahead as she had travelled on the train to London.

I'm doing the right thing, they would never understand, she kept repeating to herself like it was a mantra that helped keep her motivated. Though looking around her, Tracy did not feel as confident as her thoughts told her to. Her parents in Ireland did not know of this trip across the sea. Tracy had explained to them that she would be working overtime and her weekends would not be free to come home for awhile to them. Her sister in London had a room in the nurse's home, which was attached to the hospital Sally worked in. God, thought Tracy wont Sally get a surprise to see me.

Now, close to tears in the restaurant, she remembered all the brainwashing she had tried on that journey over. How getting her ticket for the underground, Tracy had stood on the platform feeling mixed up, alone and frightened. She had counted the stops on the wall map to Oxford station and the journey in only took twenty minutes.

When going up the escalator on to the street, she took in the scene that was before her. People everywhere, briefcases and mobile phones, newspapers stands, street sellers and traffic. Then, standing in the centre of London and without warning a rush of excitement had swept through her. The colours and sounds that wrapped around her were intoxicating. The cries of the street sellers, the music from ghetto-blasters, the blare of car horns and the buzz of so many people crossing each others paths, it was wonderful.

Tracy looked at the tall buildings and took in the well known names and realised she was holding her breath of this large city. "The Steakhouse" had appeared welcoming and Tracy headed for the restaurant. Minutes later she was enjoying a salad of mixed greens and cold slices of roast beef, it was delicious. So now, a little more relaxed after eating her meal, Tracy sat sipping her glass of juice.

She rose from the table and strolled out on to the streets, undecided of where she was going, she leaned against a litter bin, watching the rush of the crowd before her. What was I thinking of to come here? So many people, so many faces all rushing about, not one smiling, just head down. Automatically she placed a hand on her tummy, she knew the reason.

Thinking again about home, she felt she had no choice. A baby would be difficult to rear on her own in a flat, her parents would be devastated with the news, their daughter, their youngest daughter pregnant, never! She now opted to phone Sally and see what help she could offer to Tracy. With the deepest of breaths and fingers crossed Tracy found a red phone box and slowly pulled out the crumpled paper with the hospital number on it. Without waiting to have another thought, she dialled the numbers and in seconds the dial tone had changed to a ringing sound. A few moments later she was put through to the ward her sister was assigned to.

"Hello Sally" she spoke with hesitancy.

"Why Tracy, this is a surprise. Oh Lord Trace, what's wrong? Is it Mam? Dad?"

"No, no, Sally, their fine, everything is great at home. Me, it's me, I'm in London and I, I need help".

The silence that followed started to eat in to Tracy and yet she felt comforted by her sister's voice. A comfort that threatened more tears, taking all the strength in her heart, Tracy found her voice and broke the silence.

"I've made a mess of things; I really need your help Sally. Please say that you'll help"

"What mess are you talking about Tracy? Calm down a little. Are you on drugs? Have you had an argument with Mam or Dad? You're not pregnant, are you?" Sally's voice trailed off.

"Yes I'm pregnant", Tracy rushed in, "I can't keep it, I've got to, well you know what I mean, I thought you might help me make arrangements for a, a termination."

"Hang on Tracy, what are you thinking? There are other options you know" her sister gushed with pleading in her voice.

"It's not your decision, look, listen to me; I wouldn't be able to cope with any other way. You know me Sally, I wasn't able to tie my shoelaces up to recently" Tracy said half heartedly trying to lighten the tension that had swamped the conversation.

"Look Sis, I really need your help" now Tracy's tone had become serious.

"No Tracy, I'll not have a part in an abortion but", Sally added in a gentler way, sorry now for jumping at her sister. "But, meet me later after I finish this shift and we can chat about things better then .Okay? Do the folks know? Is there anyone else here with you? Tracy I can't really stay on much longer okay, but we will meet later yeah?" There was no reply from her younger sister, only quiet sobbing at the other end of the phone.

"Tracy, you listening to me pet?" Sally continued, "Okay, you are scared right now and not thinking straight so let's see if we can come to a better decision? Are you there Tracy? Don't be foolish and rush in to anything. I'll ring your mobile when I finish and we'll meet up"

"I don't have my mobile with me Sally", she whispered. Tracy's thoughts were on automatic and had slowly mentally tuned out much of Sally's long speech. She did not want her mind changed, all she needed was support and Sally wasn't going to give that without conditions attached. So with a sigh she put the phone down.

Feeling abandoned by all, Tracy stood in the phone box. She was desperate and very alone. Stepping out once more in to the stream of nameless faces, it would be easy to disappear in the mass of bodies around her. One could go missing and if they wished it, never be found. Only Sally knew she was here. It was a tempting thought, just another name on the police 'missing persons' files.

Wearing her jeans and a short jacket, Tracy looked no different from the many girls around her in the street. Her brown hair tied neatly back and carrying only a hold-all bag, who would really notice her among the crowd? Wise up lady, she heard a voice in her head tell her. Your family would never cope with a shock like that. It's a selfish and cruel thought, the voice continued. Lately she had lots of doubts about the decisions she was making.

Life had changed so much for her in the past year. Moving to Dublin at nineteen years old having got a job in one of the large advertising agencies and now this!!

It was then she thought she saw him. The man had his back to her but there was no mistaking the blonde hair cut tight into his head and the denims he always wore, the collar turned up. How could he be here she thought puzzled, her Liam here in London, not possible! Her hazel eyes never left him, she could see he was laughing, his shoulders shaking gently. Who is with him? She felt dizzy, it was all too much, and it's just not possible. Her eyes were definitely playing tricks!

He then started to move away, throwing his arm around a girl. Instinctively she followed them. Walking behind the couple in the street, she watched them sauntering together, arms around each other. Anger and hurt rose up within her.

Remembering how Liam had laughed at her when she told him of the pregnancy. How he had said she was stupid to think he loved her and he continued to tell her to grow up and look around her. He was not committing himself to anyone or anything. It was her problem he had told her and Liam had walked away leaving Tracy shattered and facing the world on her own. Reeling from this memory Tracy sat down on a nearby bench, she felt weary. Yes she thought I was stupid, stupid to think that the first man who had smiled and paid attention to me, that I had given him my heart so willingly.

Sighing heavily she watched him turn to face her, it told her what she already knew, it wasn't him, her Liam, and he disappeared into the crowd.

"Go on you bastard" Tracy screamed and slumped on the seat in tears while those around her muttered about drugs and crazy young ones. Let him go she mumbled to herself, just like I'm letting go of this baby. Jolted back to reality by this sobering thought, she gently stroked her tummy.

"It would never work" she whispered softly to her child, it was all a mistake. She looked around her and got back to her feet, time was wasting. Casting a glance in the direction the young man had gone, Tracy knew she secretly hoped that Liam would follow her, saying he loved her and they would rear their child together. What had occurred just now was an illusion of her broken heart.

From Oxford Street she had followed the stranger on to Tottenham Court road, now Tracy was worn weary after the day's events. Glancing up at the pub ahead of her, she smiled to herself.

It was called "The Last Stop", it felt to her like a good place to gather her thoughts. Sitting down, she ordered a vodka and tonic. Tracy knew that drinking while pregnant was not a good idea. But did she now really care? Tears stung her already swollen puffed eyes and she once more allowed them to fall. Out of her pocket she took the paper with Sally's phone number and below it the phone number of a London clinic.

The anxieties of the past few weeks flooded her mind and her heart ached for her unborn child.

"I'm sorry baby, I really am, and it just wouldn't work" Was she as Sally had said, not thinking straight? Was she or had she really got other options open to her? Looking at the two phone numbers on the battered piece of paper, Tracy tried to decide and knocked back the bitter drink she held. Clutching the empty glass and taking a deep breath she glanced at the phone box outside. Her decision was made and she ordered another vodka and tonic from the friendly bartender.

****

THE COFFEE MORNING

Rachel was the first of the women to arrive. The morning was a fresh one, no wind just crisp cold air to wake one up. Once a month Rachel and her three friends met at the local café to catch up on each others lives. This coffee morning was an important meeting for Rachel; she was bursting to share her news. She had arrived early to settle herself. She liked to sit facing the café door. It meant she could view all who came in and so she would be prepared for any surprises. Rachel had been reading about Feng Shui. Never sit with your back to a door was a golden rule. Ever since learning about the how's and why's of the Chinese practice, Rachel paid more attention to her surroundings.

Although Rachel was totally absorbed with her new interest, she was driving her friends crazy with constant talk of chi channels, mirrors, reflecting energy and general placement of furniture and such. In fact Rachel had bored them with details but her friends waited for this hobby to pass over. Before Feng Shui Rachel had obsessed with cross-stitch and so each of her friends had received cross-stitch bookmarks, pictures, even mini cushions all as presents. Of course the girls all oohed and ahhed at the appropriate times and Rachel had beamed with pride.

Then she had a phase of dried flowers arranging which resulted in bunches of twigs and flowers being shoved in all sorts of containers. It was the new rustic look Rachel claimed. Then all the dried flowers had to go when Feng Shui walked in the door. All that negative energy was unstable to say the least. Rachel wasn't married. This was a blessing the others remarked as what man could put up with all the crazy hobbies Rachel enjoyed pursuing.

"Olive over hear!" Rachel waved at her friend as Olive pushed open the door.

"Great to see you, I love your hair" Olive hugged her friend warmly. "Have you ordered?"

"No, just here five minutes. Any sign of the others as you were coming in?"

"Sharon text me last night to say she would be running late this morning. She forgot young Jamie had the dentist. So she will get here in bout half an hour I guess"

"Poor Sharon always running after her kids, how she does it I don't know", Rachel pushed her auburn hair behind one ear.

Olive was married six years to Tim. They both had busy careers which often meant she and Tim would pass like ships in the night and only communicate by phone calls. A small smile teased at Olive's mouth, she too had news to share but would wait until they were all together. Rachel and Sharon had discussed Olive's lifestyle at length and wondered why Olive had bothered marrying at all. She spent so little time with Tim it wasn't a proper marriage, was it?

Maybe that was the secret of a happy marriage Sharon often thought when picking up her Jacks trousers from the floor each day, or rinsing the sink after he had left his shavings stuck around it. Yeah, that must be it Sharon thought, be too busy to be together and just talk by phone, have a cleaner come in and deal with the household side of things. Jack may be a trifle lazy around the house but she knew he loved her. What did Tim get up to on all those business trips, it was this little nasty thought kept

Sharon sane as she went about another days monotonous housework.

"Look, here comes Cathy" The two women waved over towards the door.

"What a lovely morning, I decided to walk, get some exercise in" Cathy took off her pale blue jacket and placed it on the chair near her.

"Sharon will be here later, so will we just order a coffee until she arrives?" Olive stood up and faced the two friends, "Ok two coffees and a tea yes?" she continued. The others nodded.

"I love the jacket, where did you get it?" Rachel enquired as Cathy settled herself.

"The new boutique in Cecilstown, it had some great opening offers and I couldn't resist", Cathy loved fashion.

"What about your hair, the style is amazing, when did you change it Rachel?"

"Two weeks ago. Decided it was time for a complete spring clean of my wardrobe and home, its good therapy to de-clutter you know ladies" Rachel spoke as Olive placed the tray she had on the table.

"What are we talking about?" Olive put the mugs out and sat down.

"Rachel's hair" offered Cathy as she poured the milk.

"It's fantastic I know" Olive said while giving Rachel an admiring glance.

"When I was clearing the house I said to myself why not change the way I look too!" Rachel swung her head so the auburn locks fell gently by her face.

"So how's Tim? Away or at home?"

"He's fine. At home at the moment, he is thinking of cutting back on the away trips. Not getting any younger you know".

"Well none of us are when you think about it," Rachel was in a thoughtful mood. She wished Sharon would hurry up and get here. Just as she sipped her tea, she heard her friend arriving. Sharon always made an entrance without meaning to. It was just her way, so used to rushing after the children, Sharon didn't ever slow down. So wherever she went she was like a mini-hurricane.

"Well ladies what have I missed? Sorry for being late, usual excuse!"

"The kids" they sang in unison.

So now the chatting could really start. They ordered some fresh tea and coffee and home-baked drop scones. The women had been friends for years and their monthly date for coffee and chat was sacred. It was rare for one of them to miss the morning. They would tease Olive that she saw more of them than Tim. Sharon used the coffee date to stay sane. If she heard another word about school runs or sports bags she'd scream.

Rachel needed to try out her new ideas on the long-suffering women. Cathy had a problem with cash she never had any!

So these coffee mornings kept her grounded. Her friends knew to tell her when to stop the spending sprees. In fact it was these great friends that had taken her credit card and chopped it in two before her very eyes. Eyes that had filled with tears that day, tears of gratefulness that someone had cared for her. Sharon had gone to the bank with her and helped get her affairs in order. Now Cathy's credit-card debt was almost cleared and she only dealt in cash.

"So any scandal then? Anyone got something juicy to share?" Sharon loved to hear stories about the outside world as she called it. Being a stay-at-home Mum often meant busy boring days of house routine.

"Did you hear about number 46?" Olive offered as she smothered her scone in blackcurrant jam. The air hostess one I've told you about. She and hubby are moving. House being repossessed. Sign of the times" Olive sighed. "It's a shame he was quite good-looking too!"

"Olive you're a married woman!" the others laughed.

"This recession is really hitting hard". Sharon was thinking of the new sports gear her eldest lad needed, not to mention the next school term fees.

"Ha recession, I've been living in a recession since ye cut up my credit card" Cathy said sadly and looked at those around the table. Again they all burst out laughing.

"So what are the plans for the next few weeks anyone." Rachel sipped her tea.

"I want to see that new Jennifer Anniston film, any takers?" Cathy wondered.

"Great Id like to see that too." Olive offered, "Would next Thursday week suit you, I'm around then" Cathy nodded.

"I've got some news" Rachel blurted out.

"What now?" Sharon teased her, "Hand gliding? Pottery classes?"

Rachel didn't mind, she knew her friends meant well. They all looked at her waiting for her to spill the beans. Rachel drew a deep breath, she felt clammy and her friends noticed her going pale.

"You Ok pet? You can talk to us, is it work? Your parents? Cathy held Rachel's hand as she spoke softly.

"I'm pregnant"

"You're what? But how?" Olive exclaimed.

"Ah, Hello Olive, I think we know how "Cathy blurted at the woman across from her, "the question is by whom?"

"Well," Rachel wanted her friends to be happy for her, "remember the guy I said I was seeing a few months now, Jonathon, well, he is the Dad"

"Is this what you want?" Olive enquired, "I mean Rachel, this is a huge step".

"I'm thrilled really. Once I got over the shock, I'm really happy. Like we said earlier, we are not getting younger and well now that I am pregnant, I'm thrilled"

"What about Jonathon?" Sharon wanted to know, the remains of a buttered scone disappearing into her mouth.

"He is thrilled too. We've discussed it, no getting married, yet, but we'll consider moving in together after the baby's born"

"Congratulations Rachel. Once it's what you want and you are happy, then we are too, right girls?" Olive raised her coffee mug in the air to toast the good news.

"So anymore wonderful revelations while we are here?" Sharon enthused.

"I've got a bit of news too" Olive whispered, "nothing as wonderful as Rachel's but, well, it's about me and Tim"

This is it, the others thought. They are splitting up. It was on the cards really, after all what kind of relationship could survive never seeing each other. The table went quite as Rachel, Cathy and Sharon waited for Olive to tell them what they believed they already knew.

"Tim and I are taking redundancy from our jobs and we are starting up a spiritual retreat centre". Olive looked at her friends faces. They were in shock, if only she knew what they had been thinking!

"Are you serious?" Cathy was the first to find her voice, "I mean, really? A retreat centre?"

"I know, it's a big change but Tim and I were talking lately and we are always so busy that we decided enough is enough. So we've been looking into the idea of a retreat centre and we have found a premises and Tim's done courses, etc, so it's all systems go!".

"There is certainly a need. I mean how many busy people like you and Tim would love the chance to recharge the batteries". Rachel hugged Olive sitting beside her.

"Another toast ladies?" Cathy raised the mugs once more.

"To Olive and Tim" they once again raised their mugs.

"What a morning" Cathy looked at Sharon and wondered what she had to tell them.

"Don't look at me", Sharon knew that look from mornings long past.

"It's been great, so out with the diaries and pick our next coffee morning", Olive ordered the others.

They counted four weeks from now and each of them marked the next morning to meet at the cosy café. Rachel arranged to meet Sharon soon to get the full low-down on pregnancy. Olive was happy her friends approved of her new adventure with Tim. It had been such a big decision, the past six months had taken their toll on their marriage and they both knew a change was needed or they would drift apart.

Cathy had news too to share but it could wait until the next coffee morning. Seeing Rachel glow with happiness about her pregnancy and Olive beaming about spending more time with Tim it was nice to see her friends happy with life. Yes Cathy could wait, after all her doctor had said her results wouldn't be back for another two weeks and it was only three weeks since she had discovered the lump in her breast.

****

A FAMILY BROKEN
JULIE

Hell on earth is how Julie saw living. Of course it hadn't always been hell, out there, somewhere, there was proof that once she had a happy life. Finding an empty spot Julie sat down on the timber park bench. Breathing in the sunshine, letting the warmth reach into her body and caress her bones felt good, almost comforting.

The park was busy today; it was Sunday. Picnics were shared; children played at the playground, lovers lying together soaking up, all the day had to offer. But Julie knew that no-one looks deeply, just a glance she thought is enough. Once upon a time, she too was guilty of not wanting to know, ignorant of others suffering, the pretence for the neighbours that all is wonderful, it was so easy to do.

Pain washed over her heart as she watched the little girl of four maybe five years play with a doll. Julie's daughter Lorna loved playing *Mommies* too. Lorna would hold her favourite doll close and sing it lullabies just as Julie had done for her. At night, Lorna would tuck the doll into a small cot and kiss it goodnight, all the things that Julie had done for her. Where is she now Julie sighed? The tears welled in her eyes. It's all my own selfish doing, Julie knew as she turned away from the little girl in the park.

Slugging a drink from the plastic bottle she held, Julie felt lonely. The colourless liquid was bitter but numbing. It took the pain that speared through each limb, each muscle, and each nerve away for just a little while. But that was only the physical pain. The emotional baggage that Julie carried within her grew heavier each passing day. Losing her daughter all those years ago was agony. She was now with her Dad.

But it had been Julie who was responsible for taking Brian away from them all. Recalling the accident was heart shattering. Julie and Paul were shouting and throwing those by now familiar harsh words at each other. Brian had run out of the house to get away from the rowing between his parents. He had just turned seven at the time, Lorna only four years old. Paul pleaded with his wife to seek help, it was post-natal depression she answered, and it was drinking gin each day he said. He was right.

The argument lasted longer than the normal rows. Brian ran out and the little boy had sat under the tractor. He sought safety behind the large wheels, his hands clamped over his ears. His parents so busy throwing insults had not noticed him missing. Banging the door, Paul left the house in anger, he jumped up onto the tractor and Brian had died.

In the following months Paul sold the farm, took Lorna and started a new life. Julie drank her gin, her excuse now the death of her son, another day it was the break up of her family, sometimes the loss of her home. Always a reason to have a drink, the reason to stop had not yet been found.

Julie looked at all the happy families and wondered is that how it would have been for her while putting the plastic bottle to her lips. She looked so innocent to any passer-by. But looking close enough one could tell of Julie's homeless existence, the dirty shoes and the wrinkled clothes. Her uncombed hair and the smell of unwashed flesh, the pain in her eyes and the shake of her hand, the sign of all is not well. It was hell on earth.

__PAUL / LORNA__

Pulling into the cobbled stone drive, his daughter waved happily from inside the sitting room window. A miniature of her mother, as she smiled with green eyes shining and blonde hair tied up in a pony tail. Lorna loved to dance; a scarlet tutu pranced around the room as Paul now leaned against the door frame.

With the music blaring Lorna was lost in her own world. Hands held high she twirled and jumped as the music took her on a wonderful journey. Looking at his little girl in her red tutu had made Paul think of tomatoes so it was bolognaise for dinner. Of course he wouldn't dare tell her that. He headed into the kitchen to prepare dinner.

He could do with a beer but he had made a conscious decision not to drink when alone with Lorna. She came first. Was it really four years since Julie and he split? Most definitely!! That day was forever etched in memory. How could he forget the day he left her, the woman he loved, had married, lying on their old couch, a gin bottle on the ground and Julie asleep from its affects.

Lorna was now a year older than Brian had been when he died. His death had changed life completely for the family. Lorna sat at the kitchen counter while Paul took the garlic bread from the oven.

"Remember you promised a trip to the movies after my school concert Dad"

"What time is this dance concert on then?" Paul sliced some garlic bread.

"Seven thirty Dad but I've to be there for seven. Is Nan coming?"

"Of course, would she dare miss it? Is there anything I need to get for you or have you and Nan got it all under control?"

"All under control" the young girl smiled at her father but there was one thing she longed for but dared not ask him. She missed her Mum. Each night she said a special prayer that God would find her Mommy.

Up high on a shelf in her bedroom was a row of dolls that she no longer played with. After they had left her old house, Lorna didn't want to play with her dolls anymore. Lorna missed the songs her Mum sang to her when tucking her into bed. She missed her Mum brushing her hair each evening, telling Lorna that she was her little princess.

But Lorna never told this to anyone. Her Dad always looked sad when he took down the photograph on the kitchen window of the four of them. He missed Brian, Lorna knew, but she did not know if he missed her Mum.

After Brian's funeral, a lot of adults had whispered about her Mum having an illness, that she was fond of drinking. She remembered too, Dad telling her Mum, that if she really loved her family she would not drink anymore.

But Lorna's Mum did not stop drinking. That's what made Paul sad and hurt Lorna most.

"Hey, scallywag why so quiet? Nothing to tell your old Dad this evening"

"Can I have some ice-cream Dad?

"Yeah go on, why not, it's a Friday night, lets chill out" Lorna hesitated as she swung around on the high stool,

"Dad, why don't you drink beer? Other Dads have beer on Friday nights not ice-cream" Lorna looked at Paul and held his gaze. A silence crept into the kitchen, it felt cold, like someone opened an outside door and a draught blew through the room.

"Don't like beer honey," Paul said haltingly.

"Is it because you have an illness like Mum?"

"No pet, it's not like your Mum. I just don't like to drink on my own at home, that's all"

"But you're not on your own Dad, I'm here" Lorna pushed a little further.

"I mean without other grown-ups around pet, why the questions then?"

"No reason, just asking," the young girl had taken the ice-cream from the freezer. It was banana flavour. Paul ate the ice-cream and watched his daughter. It was unusual for Lorna to mention her Mum's drinking. He worried at times how to explain to Lorna the truth about the break-up. How it was a combination of things, Julies drinking played its part but he had never explained to Lorna how it had destroyed their lives in so many ways even before Brian's death.

Had he done the right thing by taking Lorna and leaving Julie? Should he have tried harder? Worked harder at getting Julie help? These and many other questions had tortured Paul long into the lonely nights but Julie did not want to be helped. Paul knew this. In fact her counsellors had reassured him, he had helped her in every way he could but until she wanted to accept help, it wouldn't work. There had been many failed rehab stints, time after time.

His regret lay with Brian, his darling son that he had crushed with the tractor. Brian's face was the last thing he saw as he closed his eyes to sleep. His son's screams as the wheel had crushed him echoed in his mind as he entered the same nightmare each night. Paul reached out and stroked Lorna's blonde hair. They smiled at each other and continued to eat their ice-cream.

BRIAN

Heaven was good. Everyone talked to everyone. There were loads of children here, different ages and all of them happy. It was a funny kind of happy though. It had taken Brian some time to understand why he was happy yet he wasn't with his family. Brian's Guardian Angel was very good to him, when he came to Heaven.

His Angel's name was Rocky. This really surprised Brian because he thought Rocky should have a name that sounded holy or more like a saint.

Rocky really was his best friend. Any questions Brian had, Rocky would sit with him and help him find the answers. Rocky also brought him to meet other children so Brian wasn't alone. When the children were together, they told stories about their earth life. But the stories didn't make the children sad even though some of them had been very sick and others like Brian had had accidents. No, Heaven was a happy place and soon Brian was settled with his new friends and Rocky.

One day Brian had felt a funny feeling in his tummy. It was just like he used to feel before his football game on Saturdays. His Mum told him that he had butterflies in his tummy, that it was ok, he was just nervous. But now here in Heaven with Rocky, the funny feeling was happening and Brian wanted to know why he was nervous? Rocky smiled and put an arm around Brian.

"What you are feeling is your earth family asking you to help them. They are thinking of you and when that happens' you feel it in your tummy." Rocky explained.

"And can I help them?" Brain asked as he thought of his Dad and Mum and Lorna.

"Of course" Rocky said excitedly, angels loved to help people but they can only help when they are asked to.

Over the next few days, Brian sent thoughts full of love and kindness to his parents. He always sent a big hug to his sister Lorna each night just as she fell asleep.

Brian recalled the day he ran out of the house and hid behind the tractor wheel. The shouting was awful. Dad had been cross with Brian's Mum. Even some of the boys in school had teased him about his Mum.

They said she was always drunk and had laughed at Brian in the schoolyard. They threw stones at him and shouted "Drunken Mommy, drunken Mommy" as he went past them.

His parents shouted a lot at each other he remembered, especially when Daddy came in from the farm and Mommy was asleep again on the armchair or the dinner had burnt while she slept.

Brian had learned how to give his younger sister crackers and cheese and milk too so they wouldn't be hungry. Some days when his Mommy didn't drink they would go for picnics and other times his Mum would sing songs and tell them stories. But then Mommy started to drink more and she would go to a special hospital but they could never make her better because she would soon be drinking again.

Mommy was good at secrets. She would hide bottles in different places and tell the children that it was a secret place and they couldn't tell anyone.

The day Brian died, his Mum and Dad were fighting and it was his fault so Brian believed. He had told Daddy about Mum's secret places because he didn't want a drunken Mommy anymore and the boys in school wouldn't call him names. He ran out to hide because his head was hurting from the shouting.

Rocky explained to Brian that nothing was Brian's fault. His parents knew this too and that Brian would understand it all in time. Rocky really was a good friend and soon Brian did understand.

So every night he sent his sister a hug and his Mom and Dad a loving thought just to help them.

****

ALWAYS A CHOICE

Joe listened to the morning radio show while buttering his toast. Wholemeal brown bread with low fat butter and two scrambled eggs and fresh orange juice were set before him on the marble counter top. It was important that he ate healthily. Now dressed in navy chinos and check shirt with black slip-ons, he was nearly ready for the day ahead. Just one more deed to do before work and then he would be set to join the many commuters that were already packing the buses and trains to the city.

Another day just like the one before, nothing new, same routine, same everything. It really was a boring existence and Joe was never so glad to have it this way. This was the first time in a long time that he had felt safe. What was more important was that he could once again face himself and know he was a lucky man. Each morning Joe looked in the mirror and said a silent prayer for the man he was staring at. It felt even good to shave. The warm water splashing on his face, the soap soft and the clean feeling it left him with. His hair was starting to show some grey, just a little here and there. He didn't mind really it was going bald that he had issues with.

"Hey Joe, how's it going this morning? You missed a great party last night. Rob from administration was doing stand up and was really great" Sarah informed him as he sat at his desk.

"Had an early night, just watched a DVD and took it easy" he replied as he checked his diary for today's appointments. Sarah and he shared an office and got on really well. Sarah was recently married and busy setting up her home with her new husband. It was a busy day, phones ringing, meetings held and meetings cancelled, lunch just a sandwich grabbed while at their desk.

The mornings Joe got a bus to work but he always walked home from the office no matter the weather. He lived three miles away in the smart part of town. His apartment was in a much sought after block and although he was financially well off, he did not own a car. By walking home each evening it gave him time out to gather his thoughts, to think about any issues that niggled him plus with no-one waiting for him at home, he was his own boss. On the walk home by the local park he watched the families feed the ducks or the children play in the playground. Guilt would tap him on the shoulder.

Other times he would sit in a café that served the best coffee ever he believed and while there he would browse through the evening paper. The waitress Anna, knew him now and would just nod towards a table and bring over the coffee. It was nice to be considered a regular and on occasions Joe treated her to a gift certificate just to acknowledge her thoughtfulness. Sarah often teased him about the waitress and asked him why he didn't ask her out.

He laughed off the suggestions but lately he wondered was he ready to share his life with another person. More importantly was he ready to share his past with another or would he be risking too much. It hadn't been easy for him to get back in the game of life. Every ounce of strength and will that ran through his blood had been drawn on for him to make a full recovery. Discipline had played a crucial part and when Joe felt tempted to cave in and go back to the old days he would step up on his treadmill and pound his way to thinking right again. Four years had passed since he got the job at the advertising company and it was the following year that Sarah had joined.

    The counsellor had been very helpful in Joe's effort to start over after what he called the dark years. How much he had lost during that time and could never get back. Family, friends, jobs, reputation and most of all his dignity he had forfeited through his own blind foolishness. When he had finally been arrested, it had come as a relief. He so wanted to be put away for life and the key to be thrown in to the deepest ocean. But a deal had been struck and it was arranged for an undercover operation to be set up and the main people behind the whole sordid nasty life to be caught. Joe had been offered a new identity and relocation to a foreign shore but he refused both. He was prepared to take all that was coming to him.

    His introduction to drugs came via the party route, sniffing cocaine and passing a joint was all part of the evening but Joe craved more. He thrilled at the high he got from mixing drugs and drink. It wasn't long when the whole lonely scene had sucked him into its depths but Joe was not near the lowest he was yet to sink in this life that was hell.

Soon he needed help to fund his habit and even becoming a dealer didn't satisfy the financial debt that clouded over him each day. It was while he was at Hell's door that he was offered a solution. Joe had been desperate, yes; he was recruited when at his lowest but nothing could excuse what he had carried out. Joe would argue he had no choice and that was why he agreed to scout for homeless children for trafficking but there is always a choice.

The police set up the undercover operation using Joe as their contact and it took six months for it to come together. Often now Joe still jumped at a knock at the door or a hand on his shoulder. He could never forget the day he waited in his old flat for the main man to call. Two hours before the knock on the door he had been dreading it. The sweat was dripping from him in fear, his hands shaking, and his voice a nervous squeak. But he pulled it off and the police got their man and Joe got a reduced jail sentence.

"If you stare any longer at the cup I'm going to wonder what's in it!"

"Sorry, what did you say?" he snapped back to life in the café and found Anna standing by his table.

"Hard day at the office" she smiled as she gave him a refill of steaming coffee.

"Just in my own world" he blushed as he thought how silly he must sound.

"It's nice there isn't it? In your own world I mean. I love to curl up on my sofa and grab a glass of wine and just drift in my own thoughts" she said dreamily while pulling up a chair near by and joining him. Joe checked the time on a giant wall clock behind the café counter. He had been sitting here for almost an hour. He noticed there were only a handful of customers at present.

"Quiet here tonight" she blurted as if she had read his thoughts, "Hope you don't mind me resting my legs for five min's do you?"

Joe smiled and welcomed the intrusion. They chatted until it was time to close up the business and it was agreed that they would go to the movies the following Thursday. Things had moved quickly but Joe and Anna enjoyed the time they spent together. Life had a new buzz in it and Joe admitted to Sarah that he was really attracted to Anna and maybe he was ready to get serious about the relationship. Life continued with the usual routine of work and evenings out and the fear of his past that haunted Joe began to slowly dissolve into a faraway fog.

Sarah announced her pregnancy early on a Monday morning to Joe. They headed over to the café to share the good news with Anna at lunch time. Anna offered to host a party the following Friday at her place in celebration of the happy event.

Sarah was the closest Joe had to family now, having lost the trust and respect of his parents and siblings over his past. But now he not only had Anna in his life, he had the added bonus of being Godfather to Sarah's baby when it was born. She asked him at the party and was adamant, when he protested that she surely had a closer relative that she might like to ask instead, that it was him or no-one. Soon his life had taken a new turn and no longer was each day as predictable as it had once been.

Anna brought a new dimension to his routine. They socialised a lot with her friends and soon each weekend was packed with all sorts of get-togethers. Joe found the hangovers on a Monday morning hard to adjust to at first but they fell into the routine just like getting to work unshaven and arriving late did. Sarah was concerned but when she tried to talk to him about how he had let things go Joe had snapped back that it was she who had always told him to ask Anna out. His gentle manner was touchy and when mistakes were made at work, he would bang on the desk and blame it all on stress. It didn't take long for him to seek out the comfort of a long leisurely drag of cannabis. He became pale and withdrawn and soon he was missing days at work.

Sarah had had enough. She went around to his apartment and kept her finger on the buzzer until he opened the door. She headed straight to the kitchen and made a pot of tea and opened the windows to let out all the stale stuffy air. Joe sat on the sofa and watched as his friend took charge of his home. Having rustled up some scrambled eggs and toast she set the plate before him.

"Eat" and handed him a fork. He wolfed down the food and was surprised at how hungry he actually was.

"Now listen to me Joe, we need to have a serious chat and I'm going to do the talking and you my dear man are going to listen" she settled into the chair opposite him. Endless pots of tea were made and shared as Sarah listed all she saw ruining his life and where it was taking him. He tried to argue at first that she was over reacting and that he had just gone through a bad patch but no argument could deny the fact that he was now a shabby dislikeable man. Sarah held her ground well and gave him a week to pull his life off the crazy rollercoaster he was on and that included breaking up with Anna. He had his choice told to him very firmly. He either continued his latest escapades with his girlfriend or he no longer would be Godfather and Sarah would put in for a transfer to a different department, she would cut him out completely.

Joe sat in the darkness of his home for hours after Sarah had gone. No-one had shown such concern or love for him even during his dark years. There was that word again, choice, he had choices. With Anna he had been living, no, existing from day to day but his every day life with Sarah meant being alive. This chance of being part of a child's life in a good way was too important to lose. Joe knew the road he would travel down. He had two phone calls to make, the first to his counsellor from before, the other to Anna.

****

A NEW START

Trevor my darling, if you are reading this, it means I am gone! Where you ask? No-one will know. When? Three days ago. This is not easy to write but at last I did it. Make the decision I mean. Time goes by so quickly and it can make you cross with yourself because you say "I'll do that tomorrow" and tomorrow comes and you don't do it. Then you realise a lot of tomorrows, in fact years of tomorrows have past by and you still didn't do what you said you would. Well I'm putting a stop to that now. I've decided and I'm sticking to my decision. I have written three letters in all. Not that the others will understand what I've done or why. It'll be my fault, wait and see. But you, Trevor, you'll understand, you will read this and feel what it is I feel, you will see it the way I see it. You won't condemn me.

How lucky I am to have met you. That was a good day, can you remember? It was in the park, I was sitting on the bench, lost in my book. How I love my books, they were my only escape in life. I could enter new worlds where no demands were made of me. But I am wandering in thought now. Yes, I was reading and you sat down and asked me if I had a light for your cigarette. I didn't. I never smoked. You asked me what was funny. I hadn't realised I was giggling like a shy teenager. It was you. You had a navy tracksuit on and had been jogging and in between puffs and gasps for air, you wanted to smoke! We both laughed then, a good day indeed.

You became an escape for me from the humdrum life I led. We didn't meet often but our cheery waves in the park to each other had me wanting more. You wanted more too. You started to go to the library. The rest they say is history. Ours is a good friendship, a friendship that worked both ways. Yet we never became involved.

We met just to listen to each other. We are each others counsellors! What you think? Ha, ha, we saved ourselves a fortune, imagine the fees if we did attend those quack pots in their mahogany offices.

I left the other letters where I know they will be found. I had debated with myself about this letter to you. About where to leave it, I mean. But it was better to post it; you deserved to know from me not from gossip or hushed whispers in the library.

Everything is sorted. I've not left any loose ends. My passport is with me. I've plenty of cash. Silly really, don't know if I'll need it.

You saw how hard life was for me. Oh Trevor, why did I stay for so long? I wasn't living, just existing. I know many others are like me. Each day they get up and face the monotony of their daily ritual. It grinds at you, it erodes your soul, and your spirit dissolves into nothingness. Tears can fall from loneliness, even frustration, but not always will they wash away that daily grind. I never felt contented. Contentment is something I yearn for. Is that why I see life as a struggle?

You always said I was a bird with clipped wings, I agree that was part of it. Each time I made an effort to change, a simple thing, maybe join an evening class, it would be taken from me. They laughed at my efforts. I would be wasting the teacher's time they sneered. Even the bingo! What was it? Oh yes, wasting money, their money and was I sure I could count above twenty? I could go on but why waste my precious time writing to a dear friend to tell you what you already know.

The power battles are over! I no longer want to play them. I am tired. It is pointless to continue. I have you to thank for that. Maybe you don't realise it, but you opened my eyes to the wonderful possibilities that can come our way each day. So I did!! I saw the fool I had become. I saw the servant they had made of me. I saw how worthless my life seemed to those whom I had given my all to.

It could change I knew that. But change means not being afraid. Being brave is what is needed. "One step at a time" I heard you say, "Rome wasn't built in a day" you often whispered in my ear when we would hug each other goodbye.

All good advice and true words spoken, but I am a coward. I'm not brave enough to conquer Rome. Even though I have decided to leave my old imprisoned lifestyle, it is not the action of a heroine but the action of a promise I made. My word is my bond.

So I am keeping my promise. I am scared; scared of the unknown. Frightened of where it will take me. There are many journeys to travel by taking that one step; the physical, spiritual and even the financial. Each nerve inside me is alive with anticipation while each muscle shakes with the fear of being caught. Gosh I must sound like an inmate of some high security prison.

But my prison was of my own making on the day I said "I do". Anyhow Trevor, no more a life of negativity for me but a life full of positive promises. I've taken that all important first step, but what if I've made a mistake? What if they are sorry? What if they miss me? My warm stew that they love on a winters evening or the welcoming flames of the bright fire I light so they can toast their cold feet and wriggle their toes as the heat seeps through them. Will they remember Tuesday is bin day? Or that the washing must be sorted into whites, coloured and dark colours, that there is a different soap powder for their woollens?

What Trevor, what if I've made a mistake? Should I go back? Tell them I'm sorry, that it's just a silly moment of a mid-life crisis? Tell them I'll go to the doctor and get some tablets. I can make it up to them. I could cook their favourite meals and, and, and oh lots of things.

Deep breath, deep breath I hear you tell me. Oh I'm shaking now, the pen I hold is hopping against the page. I must control it, I must show strength Trevor. That's it! It's control, all about control. I need to feel it, to feel I am the mistress of myself, my thoughts, and my actions. That is why, to gain my life back. A life where I will not be laughed at, used, humiliated, put down in all I do or say.

I will not contact you Trevor; this is a battle I want to win by myself. After you have read this letter I would like you to burn it. A gesture of letting me go, of destroying what we shared Trevor, you will understand. So you have listened to me for the last time, I am going to find the contentment I've dreamt of. I'm putting my old life to sleep. Popping this letter into the post box shall be the dividing line between what's in the past and what the future shall bring. Thank you my friend,

Isabel

****

COAL DUST IS GOLD

Its two hours since I started to follow him. Nothing has changed. He is still in business or should that be businesses. A sly monster is what he is. I have no doubts, for I know, I know him very well. He travels a different area each day. To those not in his clasp, Henry Duggan is the friendly coalman. Almost always he is covered in coal dust, whistling as he heaves another bag of coal over his shoulder and drops it wherever the coal is stored. His blue truck is well known, he salutes while driving along, donning his grey cloth cap to the many who return his wave.

Yes Henry Duggan is well known to those who buy his coal. But behind closed doors of Duggan Coal Supplies, lies the real reason for his wealth.

I once worked with him, taking orders from customers, arranging deliveries, accepting payments, the usual office work. But Henry kept two sets of books in his office. One was for the everyday coal yard business; the other was for his money lending. Henry accepted cash only and any interest due were paid in "personal services" to him alone.

Following him today, I notice, that some of his deliveries are to the same families that owed him money in my office days. He has gone into No. 35 Haven Close, Mrs. Shaw lives there. Henry drops two bags of coal around to the back of the house. Whistling happily, he rings the doorbell and waits. Mrs. Shaw pays him for what to others is for the coal delivery. But I know this money is not for coal but to help clear her debt, her loan that she probably got out before Christmas.

I watch him count the cash, with a shake of his head; he looks at the woman standing before him. Her face is ashen and tired looking, she pleads with him but Henry is not interested. Henry is all smiles on the outside, but in his heart its cold.

This is the part of the business that Henry enjoys most, having control. Watching customers panic, seeing them sweat in fear, as they try to buy time, explain their story, ask for space. He toys with their lives. Like a puppeteer, pulling strings to make them squirm and dance to whatever tune he plays. The reason I know the cash is not for the coal is because clients must pay for the coal at his coal store. The money that changes hands at the doorsteps is always from the money lending. I take note of what I see in my notebook. I take a photo of him at the doorway.

My collection of photographs is growing. My notebook holds details of all the houses he delivers to. Some of them I know, others are not familiar to me. But what shocks me most is the new sideline he is moving towards. It is this that both upsets and disturbs me. But I shall tell you more about that shortly. For now I must continue to follow him.

He is on the move again. No.43 is next on his list. The Shanahan's live here; I am familiar with this family. I remember the time Mrs. Shanahan called to the office to pay for her coal, her eye bruised and cheek grazed. Taking her money felt so wrong but I dare not look at her as I handed her a receipt over the counter. Those bruises were Henrys handiwork; she was a month behind in loan repayments. Her husband had abandoned the family years earlier so she was easy pickings for the bullies like Henry to ruffle up, play the hard man.

Now we have moved to Blackthorn Avenue. This is a new estate, only built in the past five years. But new or not, Henry has business in every road, corner or street. He is a master in his craft. He can reel people in, vulnerable people, with his charm and swallow them up like the shark he is

When I left the office, I moved away with the strict instruction not to reveal his business dealings. It was not difficult for me to agree, as he Henry Duggan is my father. Working at the office was only for summer jobs with me; I really wanted to pursue theatre acting. I dreamed of living in the big city, my name up in lights and proclaiming the name of the play I stared in with top billing.

I threw myself into my acting. It was hard work but I loved it, taking small parts here and there, helping with any sort of theatre work, whatever it took to learn my trade. I achieved modest success; still I was a small fish in a big pond.

Unlike Henry, he was law and order in the small town where I come from. His word ruled in many areas but lately he was becoming greedy. Always careful throughout the years never to muddy his name, it was now slightly dirty. The books were kept; he had his accountant, all above board for Revenue. But now he was shifting his business interests into a new career area. It was this that bothered me, which upset me most.

Not content in owning peoples lives through his bullying and keeping his customers in fear each day of receiving a visit from him, he now was branching into selling his female customers for sex. I had been aware of his many affairs, my mother chose to close her eyes to it, and she had long given up the arguing.

Again we are on the move, now we are driving up Chapel Lane. The bags of coal are delivered with a smile. Only a few full bags remain on the trailer of his truck. He is nearing the end of his daily run. Later he will drop into the office and check on the days takings.

He will get one of the boys in the coal store to load up the truck for tomorrow's deliveries. Then he shall go into the back office and pour a brandy. Sitting in his brown leather swing chair, Henry will sip his drink and ponder on how the day went. It will be Henry who will lock up, turn off the lights, and be the last to leave the premises. Then he will go home.

I too shall go home, but to a hotel room. I will print off the photos and write up the addresses of each house he visited. I will add these to my list of others. My file on Henry is growing. He does not know I am back in town. He is not aware of my presence. My acting experience helps me with the many disguises I need to be able to follow him undetected. Little does he know that all those acting classes he paid for are now going to be his downfall!

Why am I doing this? Why am I going after the man who is my own flesh and blood? It is because I do not like what he has done too many people over the years. Money lending was bloody bruising work but it is the prostitution that angers me. Some of the women on his books are friends of mine; they are now paying back the debts of their mothers and fathers, like Tina.

I bumped into her by accident when out clubbing one night. She was quite drunk and still knocking them back with a determination to get wasted. I approached her to offer help when she spat at me, screaming that it was she who had paid for my swanky new outfit and all the comforts that came with being Henry Duggan's daughter. She fell to the floor crying, grabbing her before security dumped her out, I brought her back to my flat.

It was then that the whole horrible story of what is *Duggan Coal Supplies* was revealed. I heard how my inheritance to be was accumulated. It both horrified and disgusted me. I was determined to bring my father down. How could I stand by and watch him destroy the lives of people I grew up with, played with, and shared teenage secrets with? He had to be stopped.

So I am on my mission, back in my old neighbourhood tailing my father, building up evidence on him. His contacts, the payments, the clients he sends the girls too, all this and much more. I have recorded all his movements and built up a file. It will make interesting reading for the Revenue Commissioners or the DPP. I have no guilt, I have no remorse, and I have no feelings of loyalty to this monster. It saddens me that my mother too shall suffer but it was her choice to stick with him and live the good life from money that is stained with the blood, bruises and tears of her neighbours; of those she calls her community.

It is the start of another day and I gather my camera and notebook. I make my way to my car and drive to the coal store. Today I approach him as his daughter and greet my father with a hug. I need to get into the office and get some more evidence. As I go through his books I note the expensive trappings of his ill-gotten gains. Scattered about are mobile phones, discarded with the same easily replaced attitude he lives his life by. This man disgusts me. I walk around his desk and my eye is drawn to the framed photograph that sits in prime position on it. Beaming out at me is myself at ten years old, sitting on my Dads knee, my arms around his neck, both of us so happy. They were the good days, happy carefree innocent days and suddenly my camera and notebook feel heavy in my bag. I sit in Dads brown leather swing chair and look at the photo and sigh. Stopping him will be hard and so my tears start to fall.

****

ANONYMOUS

The clickity click of red stiletto heels stomped across the black and white tiled floor. It was the only sound that challenged the silence of Lowstown Community Library on a Wednesday morning at 11am. Heads turned to see who was the owner of the offending shoes and with harsh sighs of having their peaceful world disturbed went back to reading or browsing the dusty shelves of books.

The owner of the stiletto heels was Mandy Highcomb, mistress of Jack Stone. Twenty years younger she is, than that sleazy blob she carries on with, Amelia Hawthorne whispered under her breath to no one in particular. Amelia is senior librarian at Lowstown Community Library. Twenty five years service and proud of it.

All the members Amelia has seen through the years, you could write a book about, she often tells the junior assistant or to anyone who will listen. Which is what Amelia had done, not exactly a book but she had revealed the saucy side to what goes on in a Library, anonymously of course.

Over time Amelia grew interested in the many people that pushed open the heavy mahogany doors to her workplace. The young children of 25 years ago brought in by their mums or dads every Saturday, now adults themselves. Some with children of their own now but Amelia never married, never had children. Usually the library's members were nice, well presented people in their dress and behaviour but not that trollop Mandy Highcomb.

Looking at Mandy now, with her black mini skirt and large gold loop earrings, she certainly wasn't here for "modern etiquette" for young ladies. Amelia did not like to see the library, her library being used for illicit meetings between lovers. The nerve of that Mandy and Jack Stone to arrange their little rendezvous on her premises.

"Good morning Mr. Peters," Amelia addressed the elderly gentleman before her desk.

"Good choice on those Mr. Peters, I hear that particular author is excellent for fly-fishing tips," she added while keeping an eye on the young trollop standing by the Romance section.

"There you go sir, books stamped and ready to go, enjoy your day Mr. Peters." Amelia smiled as the gentleman strolled off with his books tucked under his arm.

Grabbing a bundle of books, Amelia hurried towards the Romance section, her flat soles not making a whisper as she glided over the tiled flooring.

"Alright are you?" Amelia turned on the charm, "Can I help you with any particular choice?" she addressed Mandy.

"What? Ah no, ah I'm ok, just browsing thanks" spluttered Mandy at the old spinster who stood before her. Mandy pulled at her red crop top and tucked some blonde hair behind one ear. Smiling, Amelia continued to sort the books on the shelves in front of them.

"You must be considering becoming a member; I've seen you in a lot recently dear" the senior librarian spoke in such hushed tones that Mandy couldn't grasp the full sentence.

"What about a member?" Mandy asked, looking blankly at this woman who had accosted her. Where the hell is Jack she thought? As the woman beside her arranged the shelves neatly.

"No my dear, I said would you like to join our library?" Amelia whispered so as not to disturb the other patrons.

"Me? Nah, books not my thing" the young girl answered. "I prefer magazines; you know fashion ones, with Victoria Beckham and other WAGS in them."

"WAGS?" asked Amelia, totally surprised by the alien words used by young Mandy.

"Sorry, got to go, meeting someone!" Mandy turned her back and with a clickity click she moved over to the Historical section.

"Hi ya babe, what kept you? I've had to listen to some old one nagging on about members" she cooed into Jack Stone's ear.

"Traffic Hun" Jack answered as he gave her bottom a gentle squeeze while pulling her to him. Mandy giggled as they hid behind Historical Fiction and embraced. Amelia was horrified. How could they? The cheeky pair had no respect for her library. Hiding in the row behind them, Amelia listened to the lover's plans of their secret meeting at Night Owls restaurant, at nine pm on Friday evening.

Enraged, the librarian went back to her desk and started to work. She quickly made a note of the secret rendezvous on a blank white post card. She would act later.

"Everything ok, Mr. Stone?" she enquired as he handed in two books on French history.

"Sorry, em, what did you say?" Jack Stone asked as he straightened his tie and did up two buttons on his crisp white shirt. His gold wedding ring gleamed in the harsh library lights.

"Ah, the French, well known for their romance and affairs whatever you call it" Amelia added as she checked the books and handed them back to him. At least he has the decency to blush, she thought. Mandy passed the desk and gave a little cough as she went by. Her short skirt revealed legs that lasted forever. Her red stilettos were yet again eroding the sacred silence of Lowstown Community Library, clickity click.

"See you next Wednesday Mr Stone" Amelia spoke with a smile as Jack let his gaze follow Mandy's firm bottom out the mahogany doors.

Amelia tut tutted with annoyance as she watched the waggle of Mandy's bottom going out the door

Wednesday evening after locking up the library, having checked the doors and windows, plugged out the electrical bits and bobs, Amelia set out for home. She had some post to drop off on her way. It was a calm evening, no wind or breeze about. Nearing the post box, she checked the batch of post in her hand for stamps and addresses. She slid the envelopes into the post box, but held the last postcard in her hands. A white postcard with a simple message typed on it. She smiled as the postcard slipped through the silver mouth of the post box. Amelia would be going out on Friday night.

At eight pm, sitting in Night Owls, Amelia sipped a glass of white wine. She had deliberately arrived early to be seated at a table with a good view as now the restaurant was filling up with hungry customers. By nine o clock on this Friday evening, Amelia had butterflies in her tummy. The anticipation of waiting for her plan to unfold was almost too much to bear. Tucking into a warm chicken salad, she sat wondering how the evening would go.

Chatting and the clinking of glasses could be heard. The setting in the restaurant was romantic, red and white check table cloths with the warm glow of candle light and gentle music in the background. Large leafy plants were placed around in strategic positions so offering discrete seating arrangements.

A short distance from Amelia at table three, sat Jack and Mandy, she giggling as Jack whispered across the table while holding her hand. The candles flickered as Jack poured more wine for his mistress. It was now ten o clock.

"JACK WHAT ARE YOU DOING?"

Mandy's glass smashed to the floor, while Jacks face flushed beetroot. The restaurant became more silent than a morgue, as diners turned to see who Jack was and what he was up to. Amelia smiled contentedly, as Mrs. Jack Stone continued her tirade of abuse at table three, while pouring wine over her husbands head.

Justice is served, thought the senior librarian as she continued to eat her meal. Another job attended to, she smiled to herself, while travelling home in a taxi. Amelia thought of the other Lowstown citizens that she had 'helped' through the years. There was young Mr. Hardy who had used her library for selling his drugs to his customers, until the police got an anonymous tip off. He was now serving eight years in Blackstaff Prison. He would thank her yet, if only he knew it was Amelia, who had done the correct thing in telling the authorities.

Then there had been the young lady who used to meet her contacts for buying stolen goods for the local thugs, who ran a 'steal to order' in the next town. That had been a difficult issue for Amelia to sort. She had known the young girl ever since her father had brought her to the library as a five year old and Amelia had been fond of the young lady. It had upset the girl's father when he found out what his daughter was involved in. The stress had brought on a heart attack for the man but Amelia believed she had to do her civic duty and inform the proper authorities, anonymously of course!

Then there was that awful man who came in to use the computers for escort agencies. Oh the shock of it for Amelia when she innocently passed by and saw naked ladies on the screen. It really had been too much and for the first time in her long career she had broken the golden rule of any library, she screamed!

"Get out, get out of here you, you, you pervert!" she hollered after the man had recovered from the shrill voice that had pierced the library walls. When she had reported the offender, recommending a lifetime ban to libraries for the culprit, to the proper authorities, it shattered her to learn it had fallen on deaf ears. Amelia was told she should have 'Net Nanny' or some other such programme installed on the computers and how reckless she had been that she had not already done so!!

In Lowstown Community Library, the following Wednesday, there were no high heels clattering across the tiled floor, no illicit meetings for Mandy and lover boy Jack.

"Mmm, I wonder" Amelia spoke aloud as she followed three teenagers to the geography section. "Can I help you, boys?" she enquired.

"No Miss thanks. We're ah, just doing research" one of the boys sniggered. She was sure they were up to no good and she could smell cigarettes off their clothes. They were about fourteen years old and much too young to be smoking. She knew her duty, back at the desk, Amelia got out three white blank postcards.

"I know their parents" she muttered as she typed a message on each postcard about playing truant from school and indulging in underage habits. They would be popped into the post on her way home. Signed?

No, they would be left anonymous.

****

IVY CLOSE

In Number 10 Ivy Close, Sally sat on the second step at the bottom of the stairs. Her weary head held in her hands, tears of total despair falling steadily onto her lap. How had the whole sorry mess got to this stage? Not knowing what to do next or where to turn. The ringing of her mobile interrupted the silence of the big house but Sally had no interest in answering it. The phone continued but yet Sally did not respond. Finally it cut off and the stillness of silence once more took over.

It was this abrupt change in sound that brought Sally to her senses. Her neck ached, her head throbbed and her eyes were swollen. She shivered in the chilly evening air as she rose from the step. Hugging herself in order to bring some warmth into her stiff body, Sally knew there was no point in switching on the heating. She had no oil, because she had no money to pay for it, no landline telephone because she had not paid the bills, a cupboard of some food, not much, but enough to satisfy the hunger pains that gripped her stomach tightly as she headed toward the kitchen.

Grabbing the kettle she filled it and started about making a cup of tea. Sitting on the counter top was the more recent batch of brown envelopes awaiting her attention. Sally knew what they contained and sighed wearily. The red ink of the branded envelopes glowed out at her "***OVERDUE***" and "***FINAL REMINDER***". Sally sipped her tea and munched on some digestives she had found hiding behind the teabags. The golden glow of the evening sun caught her eye and she stared out across the garden.

It was the one thing that gave her peace of mind. Digging the earth and weeding the flowerbeds gave her a satisfaction like no-other. Admiring the view from her kitchen window, Sally decided to put in an hours work in the garden to occupy her mind. Grabbing her gloves and hoe by the back door she headed out to soothe her troubled mind. An advert for a home help on the local supermarket notice board had caught her attention this morning and Sally thought about giving it a go, happy now that she had jotted down the phone number. Pulling at the weeds and tossing them on to the wheelbarrow Sally felt her troubles would soon be sorted.

In number 34 Ivy Close, Ethel sat sipping an afternoon sherry, well it was technically evening as the dark wood clock threw open its doors and out popped the cuckoo telling its elderly companion that it is now seven o'clock. It had been a custom of Ethel's mother, God bless her soul, to have a single glass of the finest sherry in the afternoons.

"To keep my spirit up and revive my batteries" she would tell the youthful Ethel as the deep claret sparkled in the crystal glass. This was just one of the many traditions that Ethel had taken from her upbringing and kept in memory of those happy times.

The evening sun was setting down for the night, the orange glow of the autumn evening shone across the garden. Sitting by the window Ethel admired the many colours of her hard work. Gardening was her passion. Of course now that her arthritis was slowly making inroads in all her limbs, each joint a knot of pain and discomfort, Ethel was no longer capable of maintaining the garden herself.

Holding her crystal glass up to the sunrays that spread across the room, Ethel smiled at the glistening goblet, the warmth of the dark wine bringing a satisfaction to the elderly lady as she sipped on the lovely nectar.

Ethel had enjoyed the best of education and fulfilment in her career as an accountant for her parents firm. When they died, she had held onto the business for ten years and then sold it to her competitors and duly retired on the proceeds. Ethel flicked on her heating which was at a low setting, enough to keep the chill out of the air.

Ethel was busy boiling the kettle when the doorbell rang. One final check of the table told her that everything was in place. She believed first appearances were important. On opening the front door Ethel was greeted by a young woman with a warm smile.

"Hi, my name is Sally, I phoned earlier about the home help ad."

"Oh do come in my dear, I've just put on the kettle. My name is Ethel and I'm so happy to meet you."

The two women went into the kitchen where the table was filled with pretty china and fresh scones, with raspberry jam and cream in little ramekin dishes that matched the tea set.

"Do sit down my dear and I'll just make the tea or would you prefer coffee?" Ethel asked while switching on the kettle to boil it up once more.

"Tea please, I noticed your garden on my way in. It's really beautiful. The colours are all so neatly arranged" replied Sally as she glanced around the kitchen.

To her left, an old dresser full of crockery with a pheasant pattern, stood tall against the pale cream walls. Across from it, was a large window, adorned with curtains made from cotton material with a rose print on it, tied back, to allow the view of the rear garden and inside underneath the ledge was a Belfast sink.

Ethel and Sally chatted very easily with each other and soon they were strolling around the garden admiring the roses and geraniums. They came to an agreement that twice a week, Sally would visit Ethel and help her around the house and garden. As the months passed by, the two ladies became firm friends.

Sally enjoyed a new positive feeling and decided to advertise herself as a garden help. After all, she had the tools to work with, a good knowledge of plants and she was prepared to work hard. She got offered two other gardens to maintain, one client was heading off to Italy to spend two months there due to new work commitments. The other client was going into hospital for a hip operation and received Sally's name from Ethel.

Number 10 Ivy Close was not the headache it had once been for Sally, now that she was sorting out some of her bills. There was more food in the cupboard and her clients had paid her some of her wages in advance. The post did not frighten her nearly as much any more. The only cloud in her life was her mortgage. She was well behind with payments but she knew there was no way she could maintain her home, even if she did win the lotto. She realised she might have to sell up and clear her debts and hopefully the local council might be able to house her. Sally made up her mind that she would look into the details at the weekend.

She was due at Ethel's tomorrow and on Friday she would put the wheels in motion for moving. She went to bed that night feeling more contented and some bit sad at having to leave Ivy Close. What if they relocated her in a flat? No garden!

Over in Number 34, Ethel was thinking of away to help young Sally out. The girl had revealed her financial difficulties during their gardening one evening. Ethel had been aware that Sally was fretting about something since the moment she had called in to her on that Tuesday.

"Do tell me what's bothering you Sally" the older woman had enquired as they were weeding out a new patch to get it ready for planting up. "Is it man problems"? she teased.

"Oh Ethel if only it was. No nothing exciting as that. I'm afraid that area of my life took a back seat a good while ago" laughed Sally.

"Well then?" asked Ethel.

"Have you thought about what you are putting into this new bed? Remember it gets a lot of shade."

"I'm not sure yet "Ethel replied. "Is it money?" she added as the earth yielded at her pulling and tugging.

"Ethel!" But Sally only saw concern in her friend's soft brown eyes.

"I'm sorry my dear. Forgive an old inquisitive mind. Have you any idea of what I should plant here?" she tried to change the subject, but she knew she had hit a nerve when she mentioned money.

When Sally called in to number 34, the following morning, she was surprised to find Ethel dressed in good clothes with her handbag hanging on her arm.

"Don't look so concerned," Ethel scolded her, "I do have a life you know. I may be old but I have a little business to attend to in town. The taxi should be here in a few moments."

"Sorry I didn't mean to stare, I thought I had the wrong day and well, you usually are here to chat with that's all" Sally spoke.

"I'll be returning by lunch time," the white haired lady whispered with a twinkle in her eye and a smile.

She had made up her mind that she would leave her home and garden in Sally's good hands when the time came for her to leave this life. There was no one else for the place and Ethel liked her new friend and believed that Sally would be the ideal person to inherit the home.

Meanwhile in the garden, Sally was trying to come up with a plan to earn extra money. She did not want to let Ethel down, as the elderly lady had given her a chance when she needed one. After all, thought Sally, I could have been a mass murderer or a raving lunatic when I first met her. Try as she might she could not see any way out of it. She would have to give up the home help and try for a full-time job. This thought dampened Sally's spirits and she headed for home feeling down. She would leave Ethel a note that she had a headache and that is why she left early.

Ethel had noticed that recently she had been suffering some mild chest pains but withheld telling Sally. The doctor had told her to take it easy and would keep her monitored in the meantime.

Sally put her home on the market and there had been a lot of interest over the past weeks. She did not mention all this to Ethel as the elderly lady did not look well lately. Sally hadn't the heart to also tell her that she was considering a fulltime job. She had grown very fond of Ethel and dropped in to see her regularly outside of the two set days they had agreed on.

Shortly after a few weeks Ethel was buried in her parents plot in the local cemetery. Sally was heart broken. She was now without her friend and soon she would be without her home as the day for signing the sale contract was Tuesday next.

The fateful day arrived and Sally was anxious. Had she done the right thing? Her debts would be paid, downhearted she returned to No.10 Ivy Close for one final look. She picked up her post and without paying great attention opened it forlornly.

Ms. Sally Weston, please attend the offices of solicitors O'Shea's & Murray's on Thursday the 12th at ten am for the reading of the late Ms. Ethel Connor's last will and testimony.

Sally could not believe the official letter she was holding in her hand. Ethel had left her No.34 Ivy Close in thanks and gratitude of the friendship and care Sally had shown her. Sally sat and wept for her friend, it was the start of a new beginning.

****

WOULD MOTHER APPROVE?

Sam wasn't sure if it was a wonderful sign or a sign of disaster, but Sam thought the only way to find out would be after the performance. There was an air of expectation in the audience. In five minutes the show would start and her life would be changed forever. Sam's life savings was poured into this production, it had taken her twelve months to pull it all together but the exercise had been both draining and thrilling. So why was she niggled by the events earlier in the theatre.

After arriving at lunchtime to check out all was in order, Sam had stumbled across a white feather in her office. It was nestled between two files on her desk, she had no idea how it got there but it surprised her. Her mother had always said white feathers were a visit from your angel.

Standing near the back row she watched as people took their seats, others chatting as they looked over the programme of events for the evening. It was a full house and the buzz was a happy one but that could change if the show didn't live up to expectations. Sam's mother had not approved of her artistic career and before she died, she couldn't give her daughter the blessing Sam needed.

Listening to her mother through the years, Sam had gone through one job after another but eventually her heart had led her to producing theatre. So the feather was either her mothers blessing or a warning from her angel that tonight was yet another mistake.

Sam's mother Olive O'Dea had been a formidable woman. She did not like weakness or signs of fragility in a person. Olive wanted her only child, to amount to something. That meant a doctor or a lawyer or professor, something that held sway in the community.

A solid career, not a flimsy actress or any unreliable role related to the arts. Having letters after or before your name showed discipline in learning, education, respect earned, oh how Olive O'Dea had often sung off that hymn sheet when Sam announced she had joined the local dramatic society.

Dressing up and playing at pretend did not pay the bills she would find out, Mrs. O'Dea liked to remind Sam as often as she could. That path of theatre and films were all riddled with drug abuse, eating disorders and infidelity and of course job uncertainty. Uncertain of a job meant uncertain of money.

Of course it hadn't helped Sam's cause that her father had been an easy going man. He would dutifully withdraw to his garden shed when his wife went on a rant. They were total opposites, her parents, it was her father's patience and peaceful ways that often grounded Olive's outbursts of 'knowing what's right'.

Time was moving quickly now, there was a flutter of movement behind the stage curtains. Some technician was retesting the sound system and another was signalling to him with a thumbs up or down accordingly.

To the left of the stage was a large poster. It was in eye catching reds and yellows with black print splashed across it declaring the play "Riding the Storm", produced by Sam O'Dea. That had been another torment for Sam's mother. Sam shortening her name from Samantha. It was enough of a man's world without adding to it Olive had declared regularly. Had she ever been proud of her daughter Sam wondered as she made her way backstage?

Yet they had been two of a kind in some ways. It was that same drive and determination that both women held that made Sam follow her dream and had Olive strive for the best for her daughter.

Why tonight did the feather turn up? Wasn't she nervous enough without signs or silly superstitions finding their way into the theatre! Imagine a level headed thirty four years career woman being anxious about a feather? What was she like at all? If the others in the cast and crew knew how spooked she was, they would think her crazy.

Back in her office, Sam sat down at the solid walnut desk. It was used as a prop in a past play and now had found its way into the directors office, just like the coat-stand and that's it! The feather. The bloody feather must have been part of an outfit from some other play! How else could it appear from nowhere? Without realising it, she sighed deeply. Her breathing was gentler and her mood lightened. Smiling broadly, she strode out of the office and headed towards the stage area.

"Right everyone, places please, lighting checked? Sound checked? Costumes all in order?" Samantha had a fresh spring in her step.

The MC for the evening was out front explaining where the fire exits were and the no smoking and no mobile phones rules to the audience. The play was about to begin. She could hear the applause, and she could see the house lights go down.

Not another thought would be spent on feathers, rabbits' feet, or four leaf clovers, Sam decided while she looked on from the side of the stage discreetly hidden from audience view.

The performance was going well. The actors were giving it their all, the costumes beautiful and the audience responding favourably. Tonight would be a success and Sam felt elation wash through her as the cast took their final bow before a happy cheering full house.

"Come on Sam" the leading man was calling her on to the stage to share the glory. She stepped out and on reaching centre stage; she was presented with a bouquet of orange tiger-lilies. They were her favourites and she was thrilled that the cast appreciated her hard work. Her spirits were high. It was a wonderful opening night. Gazing at her lavish bouquet, surrounded by thundering applause, Sam's face drained of colour. Her heart beat quickened and a clammy cold sweat replaced the relief that had enveloped her earlier. How was this happening? Before her eyes, resting among the flowers and the greenery was a white feather.

The play ran for three weeks and was then going on tour to other regional theatres.

Sam was busy these days. She was dedicated to her craft. Although she started work on her next production she insisted on being at each opening night of "Riding the Storm". Interviews with the print media, TV and radio kept her busy. She was burning the candle at both ends as her mother would say with promotions by day and the shows by night.

Sam had discovered some more feathers in the most unusual places as the weeks passed. She became intrigued by their presence in her life.

Having coffee with a friend, a feather would appear as if by magic. Sitting in a taxi, she found one on the car floor. Standing in the queue in her bank, one floated dreamily down in the air and landed on the shoulder of the man standing near by. Sam decided to take note of these feathers apparitions and see if any sense could be had of it. Spotting a pocket notebook with two little cherubs smiling on the cover, Sam bought it and declared it her angel book.

    Her first feather that night in the theatre office, she had been thinking of her mother. Receiving the bouquet, her parents were on her mind, wishing she could have shared her opening night with them. Sharing coffee with her friend, talking about old times, when they had been young, parents, family get-togethers. The feather in the taxi, on her way to visit her Aunt Margo, her mum's sister. The bank feather, what had been the reason? What was she thinking? Of course! The lady behind her was wearing the scent that Sam's mum had favoured. It had instantly triggered memories of Olive O'Dea.

    Back in her apartment on a rare night in, Sam sipped a comforting hot chocolate. She had lit some candles and her angel notebook sat on her glass coffee table. Her theatre plays were selling well. She now had three successful plays behind her. Not only had she directed her shows but she also wrote her own work. People were taking her work seriously and her name was spoken about with respect in the social art circles that could make or break a new playwright/producer.

She was now contemplating on setting up her own production house and offering courses on direction, play-writing and other aspects involved on threading the boards. It was all a plan for her future; it would take time and a friendly bank manager to get the idea up and running.

Sam picked up her notebook, the cute plump faces of the cherubs grinning at her from the cover. Flipping through the pages and glancing over what was written, she noticed a common thread running through all the incidents that she had recorded. Each time a feather floated into her life, her thoughts in one way or another were of her parents, in particular of Olive.

A name involving her feather experiences for her production company might work, Angel House Productions – The White Feather Company – Heavenly Playhouse Ltd – Celestial Productions – Silver Thread Theatre? It would be all night at this rate Sam reckoned with the choice of names that were popping into her head. She would leave it to her Mum to decide, Sam was now too sleepy.

Leaving the bits of paper where she had scribbled the names on by her notebook, she headed to bed. This would be Olive O'Dea's chance to give her daughter the approval that Sam craved. The challenge was issued, if Sam got one more sign about setting up her company, it would show whether Olive approved.

Days went by and Sam was kept busy. There was no time to think about company names or feathers or indeed her mother. Tonight Aunt Margo was meeting her for dinner to catch up with each other.

"Oh Aunt Margo, guess what I found today? Sam giggled as they sat in the restaurant.

"What? Another feather?" Margo enquired between mouthfuls of smoked salmon.

"My first grey hair, well two actually! I was going to pull them out but Mum always said they would just double in number to do that!" Sam recalled with fondness.

"Silver threads are what she called them" Margo murmured remembering her late sister.

"What did you say?"

"Silver threads, Olives name for her grey hairs", Margo looked at her niece and grew concerned. "You ok pet?"

"That's it, Aunt Margo! That's my sign. Mum does approve! That was one of my choices for the company. The Silver Thread Theatre" Sam beamed brightly at her aunt. This is what she had wanted and Olive had given it to her.

****

MYSTERY CUSTOMER

I look out of the window at the passing of today. It was cosy in the café. I like to sit in the corner to the right, at table three, as you come through the green swing door. From this corner you can view all that is going on, both outside on the street or inside the café, or 'The Little Teapot' to give it its correct name.

"Okay Ms. Wilson?" the nice young waitress asked me as she tidied up the table next to mine.

"Fine thank you Polly" I replied.

I like Polly, she is friendly to me. She never hurries me along when my tea is gone and I've sat here for nearly two hours. I like the way Polly wears her chestnut brown hair scooped up in a bun. "Health regulations" she told me, the day I asked her would she ever leave her beautiful hair fall down over her slim shoulders. She had the most striking green eyes, yet there was softness in them.

"You're keeping well these times?" Polly asked as she gathered up the last of the white cups and white plates from the table. She placed them on a tray that was on another table nearby.

"I'm well Polly. How are all your siblings and dear mother?"

"Oh Ms. Wilson, that bunch are grand, just driving my poor mother crazy as usual. She's dreading Easter and all the expectations it brings. Imagine it's still a few months away and my small brothers are already thinking how many Easter eggs they want!" Polly chatted away as she wiped down the glass table-top and straightened the red plastic chairs neatly under it.

"There now" she added as she smiled over to me, happy in her work. I like Polly.

Her mother is a hard working woman. Her father died two years ago in a car accident and she, Polly, had given up school at the tender age of 16 to go to work and support her mother with raising five children. Polly is the eldest. She had her dreams of being a famous painter. Her art teacher was so disappointed when Polly told her of her decision to leave school. But she didn't mind waiting on tables. She was happy to get the job. The tips were an extra bonus to her wages. It was the café's policy with customers' tips that they all be placed in a bowl on the counter and divided equally between the staff on duty of the day.

I see the couple at table five staring over at me. I am used to stares from people. I have a reputation you see. Some folk think I'm in to witchcraft. I suppose my hair is a bit scraggly and my clothes never did suit the fashion of the times. I dress for myself. I like my own company. No man or family for me. I'm not a native. In the summer I like to leave my shoes off and go barefoot. I live with nature, in harmony. I give back to the earth what I take from it. My house is half-way up on a hillside, just a mile outside the town.

Table number five are whispering. I can hear them clearly, I have excellent hearing. They are discussing my fingernails, the dirt in them and how long they are. I shake my hands over at them and they look away sharply as my multi-coloured bangles all jingle with the sudden movement. I laugh at those silly people.

I look out of the window and watch the birds gather on the telephone wires. There are three black crows, all staring with large glassy eyes at the half eaten bread roll by the over flowing rubbish bin outside.

I'm engrossed at how they watch around before one of them flies down to the pavement. He immediately starts to peck at this gift left from some human. The bread roll is pulled and poked at by the three birds who decide there is enough for them to share. Cars and trucks going by on the road do not deter them as they greedily eat up their meal.

"Are you finished there?" snaps a young waitress at me.

It's Chelsea. I don't like Chelsea. She has blonde hair with pink streaks going through it.

"Almost finished" I tell her as I place my hands around my cup.

"Don't suppose you want anything" she adds as she starts to take away my empty plate and knife. Chelsea walks away, not even waiting for my reply.

Table number two push back their chairs and put on their coats as they get ready to leave. They put a tip of five single euros on a plate. Chelsea goes over as they go out the door and lifts up the plate of coins. She puts some of the coins in her pocket and some into the tip bowl on the counter.

She thinks she is smart. Why would you call your child after a place in England, or indeed anyplace anywhere?

A child outside on the street chases at the hungry crows. They fly to safety to the telephone wires. I decide to leave.

"Thank goodness, that crazy old mad-woman is going. She's so smelly and the state of her clothes. Honestly if this was my joint I'd have her barred. Crazy old cow."

I turn to look at Chelsea. She is surprised I heard her, as she was sure she was only whispering. I have excellent hearing.

"Hey Polly, you can clean up that one's mess at table three. I'm not touching anything that's been near her" Chelsea says loud enough for others to hear. The couple at table five laugh. Polly blushes and heads over towards table three.

I do not worry about the nasty comments. Some people are born nasty and evil. Others become so as they journey through life. Greed corrupts so easily. Others are good and compassionate, they do not judge or condemn.

I like 'The Little Teapot'. I've been having my pot of tea and two brown soda scones with rich creamy butter every Thursday for a long time now. I've seen a lot of staff changes there. Some nasty, some nice.

It's Thursday again and I am approaching the café. I go in and there are only a handful of customers. Polly smiles over to me as I take off my purple woollen wrap and place it on the chair beside the seat I sit on. I am grateful of the warmth of the café on such a frosty day.

"Same as usual Ms. Wilson," Polly calls over from behind the counter, her hands full with a tray of delph and cutlery. Chelsea is leaning against the counter on the outside and seems busy filing her nails.

"Thank you Polly" I reply.

Chelsea looks up at me and turns away. The street outside is quiet too. There is a sort of lull about the atmosphere in the café today as people huddle over their steaming cups of coffee for comfort.

I stir the cup of tea in front of me and proceed to sip it carefully. I like my tea sweet, three spoons of sugar, and hot, only a little milk.

I feel Chelsea's blue eyes on my back. I do not turn to her. Her eyes are not bright and clear. A cloud hangs over them. She knows what I am capable of. That is why she dislikes me. I can see into her heart. It is black.

She comes from a good family but she is not a good person. She chose not to be.

"Any plans for this years holidays Polly?" Chelsea asks her workmate.

"Holidays? Not a hope girl. My sister started in a new school last year, so all my cash will be helping Mam out for that." Polly answered wearily.

"Well if I ever get the chance to leave this rotten place, I'll take it. This dead-end job will be the death of me. There are times I wish I could disappear off this planet," the other girl spoke harshly.

"I wish I could get a pay rise!" Polly laughed as she wiped down table six.

I look at the two young women and say to them "Be careful what you wish for." I laugh.

Polly smiled.

"Stupid old bat" Chelsea muttered.

It is a bright cheery day and it's Thursday. I have not been to the café for two or three weeks now. I have been busy in my hillside house. I have been arranging some herbs and mixing a potion of sorts. I've decided to help two people I know. I have my beliefs, I have my ways, and I work with nature.

"Ms. Wilson, it's good to see you. Have you been ill? I hope it wasn't anything serious," Polly greets me as I sit at table three. She looks tired. Her green eyes are dull, her fair skin is pale.

"I've been busy," I tell the nice waitress. "You do not look yourself child" I add.

"Well when I looked in the mirror this morning I saw the same face as yesterday" she giggled. "It's been hectic at home. My young sister has got a bad viral infection and Mum's worn out with life. You know, with just life in general."

Polly leaves me to serve at another table, while I settle into my seat. A bright neon sign welcoming people to drop in blocks my view out of the window. Chelsea brings my tray with a pot of tea, cup, cutlery and scones.

"Thought we'd got rid of you when you didn't turn up lately, still you can't kill a bad thing or so they say."

I do not look at her. It will all happen in the right time. I drink my tea and when I am finished I place the cup in my lovely deep blue brocade bag. I ask Polly if she can bring me a cup as Chelsea forgot to bring me one, I tell her.

Polly brings the cup. I pour another cup of tea and drink it. I place the cup inside my bag. I leave. I have work to do.

It is the next week. It is Thursday. I sit at table three.

"Can I take your order please?" a new voice asks cheerily.

I turn and I cannot see Polly or Chelsea in the café.

"I'd like a pot of tea and two brown soda scones please," I tell the waitress.

When she returns I enquire about Polly and Chelsea. "Oh it's a strange thing really. Chelsea has gone missing. Like she disappeared from the face of the earth. Polly is in the office at the moment. She is the new Manageress. Would you like jam with those scones?" the girl with the name badge 'Alice' asks me.

"Yes please Alice" and smile at the nice young girl.

So I still have the magic, my powers are not as rusty as I thought.

"Thank you Alice" I say to her when she brings me a small dish of strawberry jam.

"Always be careful what you wish for Alice" I tell her.

"Yeah sure" she says turning back towards the counter. "Strange one, her" she mutters. I have excellent hearing.

****

BENEATH THE SURFACE

O'Connor's Bar and Lounge was located in a small village with a bright future. The new hotel had brought business to the village and demand for more shops and better facilities followed. So as not to get left behind in the rush of progress that was in the local air, O'Connor's had started a pool tournament on Tuesday evenings. It would bring a crowd in on what often was a quiet night in the business.

There was nothing unusual about the customers in tonight at O'Connor's pub. The three old timers at one end of the semi-circle counter, Jim, Pat and Joe, sat side by side, and had done so for over sixteen years. In front of them each was a pint of the dark stuff with a distinct creamy head and set to the side of the pints was a tumbler glass each of the finest Irish whiskey. A little jug for water was near by. These three friends sat in comfortable silence every Saturday and Sunday nights and now Tuesday were added to their list. Further down the bar were some more regulars who chatted noisily about recent sporting events and results. Some of the customers sat on the high stools by the bar others leaned against the counter while sipping their drinks.

Over in the corner of the large room was the pool table. Gathered around it were two local lads having a game. There was laughter and jeering as the players teased each other about their ability to hit the balls. Of course there were also the on-lookers who watched the game with interest. The pool tournament was well on its way now. It had started a number of weeks ago and now it was at the first semi-final stage. The final would be played on a Sunday night. The top prize was a dinner for two at the nearby four star hotel with complimentary champagne. The other prizes were hampers of foods and drink plus vouchers for local shops.

Anna was happy working here. The clientele were friendly and rarely was there any trouble to be found. She was four years serving behind the bar now and for the last eighteen months she had her eye on Harry Doyle. The only downfall was that Harry didn't seem to be interested in Anna.

"Give us a pint there love please"

"Make it three Anna and a pint of cider with ice too" shouted a local as he saluted the elderly trio at the bar end.

"Thanks lad" Jim, Pat and Joe acknowledged the drink that was bought for them as the young man took his cider and joined the on-lookers near the pool table.

Harry was playing tonight. His opponent was skilful and the game was a tight affair. This was the first of the semi-finals. While Anna wiped clean the counter top she gazed lovingly at Harry as his blonde head was lowered over the games table. His right elbow held high as he aimed at the far corner pocket to sink a ball. The cue he held firmly.

She tided the beer mats and replaced the tattered and worn ones with new ones. All the time her gaze lingered on her secret prince. The shot was a success and he went on to win the game. Harry was in the final. A cheer went up and a lot of backslapping and hand shaking went on as Harry made his way to the bar.

"Can I have a beer shandy please Anna" he asked while settling down on a stool.

"It's on the house Harry" smiling shyly she handed over the pint to him.

"Thanks, that's great. It's amazing the thirst you can work up during a game" Harry spoke, raising the glass to his lips. Anna went about her work, serving drinks and cleaning up while the evening went on. Now and then she and Harry would share a few words where he sat mainly by himself.

Others would chat to him but she noticed they came to him. He never really imposed his company on others yet he was equally quiet happy to either have company or sit on his own. The rare occasions there was a fight or disagreement on the premises, it would never be Harry's hand or voice raised in anger. He had a calming tone to his voice and when his dark blue eyes looked at you, you knew he was really listening as you spoke. Conversations were never half-hearted ones; Harry gave his full attention when in his company.

It had been easy for Anna to fall in love with him. She had hoped that he would win the pool tournament and ask her to share the prize dinner with him. Each night before she slept, she would picture them sharing the meal together in plush surroundings of the hotel. It would be romantic with a candle lit and a small posy of flowers on the table. Across the flickering flame, Harry would look adoringly at her and he would reach out and hold her hand ever so gently. They would giggle as the champagne cork would pop up into the air and bubbles and fizz would tumble into the slender glass flutes. Each night she would dream the same dream but first she would have to wait for her prince to win.

    Harry Doyle knew nothing of these fantasy thoughts of this local barmaid.

    It had been a good game of pool earlier and getting to the final was a nice feeling. The simple stuff in life made him happy. Having friends and family, living each day and doing ones best never to hurt people was the motto Harry tried to live by. Recent months were a struggle for him because he had dealt with a lot of inner turmoil. Questions about the future, his future, what was laid out for him, what road he would travel, haunted him until he had gone away on a break. Taking time out had settled these unanswered questions which up till then were scattered in his head like an unmade jigsaw. If he won the tournament wouldn't it be a lovely way to finish his life in the village. People would be praising him and remembering him as a sort of local sports hero, well not hero exactly but prize-winner at least.

Harry knew too who he would give the first prize to. He had no interest in a fancy dinner, getting all dressed up in a suit and feeling foolish.

The second semi-final was held the following Tuesday. There was a large crowd in as the locals were interested to see who their Harry would be up against. Like the previous semi-final, the game was a tough fought one. The victor was a young man from a nearby town. So the village placed all bets on their own lad and the tournament took on a carnival air. Posters declaring loyalty towards Harry went up on shop windows and in the Post Office. Even the local curate wished Harry success when they met after church on the Sunday.

The proprietors of O'Connor's decided to make the competition an annual event such was the buzz it had stirred up in the area. Surrounding parishes would be asked to submit players in the future and maybe some fundraising could be incorporated over the weeks of play so a charity could also benefit.

Anna carefully applied her make-up before she started her shift at the pub and she checked herself in the mirror before she left for work. It was the night of the final and she wanted to look her best when Harry would ask her to dinner after he won the game! Arriving at O'Connor's, she saw that extra floor staff was on duty to help with the busy night ahead. Harry was in early too and looked relaxed while chatting with the other customers. All were wishing him well. Shortly his opponent with a sizeable group of supporters arrived and both finalists shook hands.

Following the event, finger food would be served to all and presentation of the prizes would take place, it was announced. The game was on; Harry had won the toss of the coin to see who would break. Stepping up to the table Harry surveyed the people around him and smiled. He wondered would he ever hold such attention again. He hoped so but would never know. A lot of sighs, cheers, and groans later, the game was ended as the black ball sank into the right hand corner. Harry was the hero.

The eruption of shouts and applause were deafening from the villagers. Anna beamed with happiness, her soft green eyes sparkling with sheer joy. She could feel her heart thumping when he walked over towards her.

"Congratulations" Anna grasped him in a large hug.

"Thanks it's a great night sure. Some of this lot will celebrate until the early hours, any excuse as it's said" Harry laughed.

"Let me get you a drink".

"Grand and join me for one will you?" he added as Anna went behind the counter to serve him.

"You will be dining in style at the hotel soon with your winnings" she teased in hope as she set the pint in front of him.

"About that Anna, I wondered, well I wanted to talk to you……"

"Harry get over here for a photograph", the local newspaper wanted a shot of the winner by the pool table with the proprietors of the pub. The night ended in a party mood and the crowd went home.

Harry was disappointed that he didn't get an opportunity to speak with Anna again after earlier.

Jim, Pat and Joe were sitting at their usual perch the following Saturday evening. There was eagerness to their normal banter. Anna came on duty and leaning against the cash register was a white envelope. Her name clearly printed on it in handwriting that she did not recognise. Still puzzled, she opened it and saw a voucher for two at the new hotel and also a short note. Anna did not understand.

"Give us a pint Anna will you. I suppose you heard about Harry heading off to Maynooth, the training place, yesterday"

"Maynooth?" Anna's voice was shaky.

"Yeah, signed up for the priesthood he has" Jim said while Pat and Joe nodded in agreement.

****

A SUNBEAM

The room is warm. There are candles lighting, they flicker and their reflection can be seen in the window. I am not alone. Linda is standing at the foot of the bed. To her left is Archie. They shift from foot to foot. It appears they are restless or maybe frightened? It's not easy for them but it is time for me to go. I want to be with my dear Norman. It's been too long without him and I know he is waiting.

"Mum you feeling okay? Have you any pain?" my poor Linda, she is pale and there are dark circles around her eyes. She's whispering to her brother and although I cannot speak, I understand what is said. I am aware of what is happening around me.

She comes closer to the top of the bed and places her hand gently on my forehead. I look into her tired eyes and think of her birth and when I brought her home.

She was five days old. Her independent spirit came through from an early age. Always asking questions, wanting to know the why's and how's of everything. She was walking by ten months, patience never her strong point.

"Any pain Mum?"

I turn my head from side to side. No pain, no feeling of anything at all. Just tired. Linda continues to stroke my forehead. Archie pulls over a chair to give to her.

"Here Linda, sit down for a bit. Will I get some coffee for us?"

She sits. I watch my daughter as she moves on autopilot. I can see her thoughts all jumbled up inside her head. She is trying to be strong. My darling who has always enjoyed a challenge is now facing a heartbreaking future without me.

It is something that has always upset me as a mother; I'm speaking about not being able to protect my babies from hurt, pain and the knocks that they must endure on their path through life.

I turn to look out the window. It is an ordinary day. The sky is a pallet of blues, the clouds like smears on glass. I can hear the buzz of life as traffic pass-by. The sirens of ambulance or police as these brave people go about their jobs. The beeping of car horns as irate drivers rush to and from their destinations. I hear the shouting of college students as they greet each other in cheerful voices. It is just another day for so many.

Linda sighs. I return my gaze towards her. She glances at her watch. It is a gold bracelet with three little jewels set into the face of it. A present for her twentieth birthday from her Dad and I. She catches me watching her and she blushes. I want to speak to her. To reassure her, 'Oh Linda, don't be embarrassed. It's ok to want it to be over'.

Dying can take a long time. It consumes all in its path, not just the victim of the grim reaper but part of those looking on too.

"Any change?" Archie is back. Two coffees and biscuits scattered on a plate, all on a red tray.

"A nurse gave these to me" I watch him place the tray on a nearby trolley. They both milk and sugar their coffees and I see their shoulders sag. They are weighted down and I watch both my children stand close to each other as they try to absorb comfort and strength from each other.

The nurses placed a fan on my locker. It keeps me cool and the whirr of its blades is soothing to me. It will spin round long after I'm gone and it will cool and comfort some other soul as it faces the final journey. How easy it is for me to let go. There is a calmness and peace in my life that has long been missing. I struggled after Norman died, we had been a complete unit throughout our marriage and so happy.

Looking at Archie I see a little of his father's ways, in the arch of an eyebrow when he is surprised, how he scratches his left palm when he is anxious. So similar yet he is his own person. Archie is a gentle soul. He loves his books, inquisitive in a quiet way. He took his lead from Linda when younger, his sister watching over him as they grew up. But here in this clean pristine room, Archie is in control. It will be he who will guide them through their grief filled future. It is he who will hug his sister, share her pain and encourage her to laugh, to remember the memories that prove painful but necessary to acknowledge, all for the days ahead.

I watch them together and think of the circle of life. What we take for granted as we go about our daily life. How we can live wrapped up in our own cocoon, reaching out only when needs must. Yet we all play a part on this great stage that is our world and make full the empty spaces that link our stories together. Little do we realise we are all in leading roles. Now it is my turn to exit, to become a sunbeam.

I wonder do Archie and Linda remember. How excited each morning they watched for the sunshine creeping into their bedrooms. Each ray of the sun a memory of those gone, their grandparents, Harry the Yorkshire terrier, other pets they had owned, each a sunbeam, greeting them at the start of the day. It was their Dad who always shone brightest; I wonder do they remember the sunbeams?

Archie is deep in thought; his eyes are easy to read. The softness of his gentle nature a light blue, yet how dark almost navy his eyes become when angry and the hard edge that appears and the coldness they can possess is alarming. But I watch him now and they are soft, he is remembering, recalling times past and his tears seep out, falling onto his chest and he approaches my bed and holds me hand.

"Mum I love you, I never said it much but I do and thanks too, for everything. We never could pull the wool over your eyes. Remember the yellow vase on the window sill? It was me. I know you knew but I couldn't admit it because it was a present to you but I didn't mean to break it".

I smile at how strange it is to hear him speak of the vase he broke when he was eight. It is like he reads my mind for now he is smiling.

"Stupid isn't it Mum?"

Now I see his tears mix with his smile and my sweetest boy bends down to hug me. I smell his aftershave, a light hint of musk.

The sun shines through the window and the rays fill the room. The nurses had wanted to pull the curtains but my children had said no. Now I see my Norman. He is standing in the room with us watching us all. He will not interfere, the love in his face as he looks towards the kids, pleased they are here for me.

"Hey Archie look at the rays, they are touching Mums bed. It's near time. They are coming for her." Linda joins her brother at my bedside.

"It's okay Mum, I love you" she whispers, "Give Dad a hug from us" she adds as she holds her brother's hand.

I feel my heart breaking. My lungs are weary and my breathing grows laboured. I look towards Norman and he nods. I smile and know it is time to leave our children and join their dad. I never imagined my death to be like this, to be peaceful and surrounded by such love. I am one of the lucky ones. The sunbeams travel up my bed and I sigh contentedly. I look at them both and smile, I turn to Norman and he reaches out his hand towards me. I smile again and close my eyes.

"Go be a sunbeam Mum," Archie speaks, as Linda's tears fall silently.

****

Printed in Dunstable, United Kingdom

70426724R00071